This book belongs to:

_____

_____

_____

Which Nose for Witch?

An original concept by author David Crosby

© David Crosby

Illustrated by Carolina Coroa

MAVERICK ARTS PUBLISHING LTD
Studio 11, City Business Centre, 6 Brighton Road, Horsham,
West Sussex, RH13 5BB, +44 (0)1403 256941
© Maverick Arts Publishing Limited 2021
Published August 2021

First Published in the UK in 2021 by MAVERICK ARTS PUBLISHING LTD

American edition published in 2021 by Maverick Arts Publishing, distributed
in the United States and Canada by Lerner Publishing Group Inc., 241 First
Avenue North, Minneapolis, MN 55401 USA

ISBN 978-1-84886-778-9

Maverick
publishing
www.maverickbooks.co.uk

distributed by **Lerner**

With thanks and
love to my family
– D.C.

For Samy and Teresa
– C.C.

Which NOSE for WITCH?

Written by
David Crosby

Illustrated by
Carolina Coroa

Grizelda is a baby witch,
She's such a pretty sight.
Her dainty little button nose
Won't give the world a **FRIGHT**.

But now Grizelda's growing up
A special day has come.
She's off to choose her grown-up nose,
A super **WITCHY** one!

She steps into 'The Conk Boutique'
And can't believe her eyes!
Rows of noses fill the shelves,
There's every **SHAPE** and **_SIZE_**!

"Now don't be shy!" her mother cries,
"Just pick a nose that's ace.
Then I shall cast my **NOSE-SWAP** spell
To try it on your face!"

Grizelda picks a pointy one,
With two **WARTS** on the end.

Her mother waves her magic wand...

Griz feels her nose extend!

"Oh Griz," says Mom, "you're gorgeous, girl!
Like something from a dream!"
"This nose is not ideal," says Griz...

"...When eating an **ICE CREAM!**"

Grizelda picks a hook-shaped nose,
It's **BUMPY** and it's **SCARY**.

Her mother waves her magic wand –
Griz feels her nose grow **HAIRY**!

"Oh Griz," says Mom, "it's beautiful!
You look **COMPLETELY** witchy!"

"This nose feels really bad," says Griz.
"It's **TINGLY** and it's **ITCHY**!"

As Griz turns down each frightful nose
A crowd appears, wide-eyed.

Mom takes her daughter by the hand,
And marches her outside.

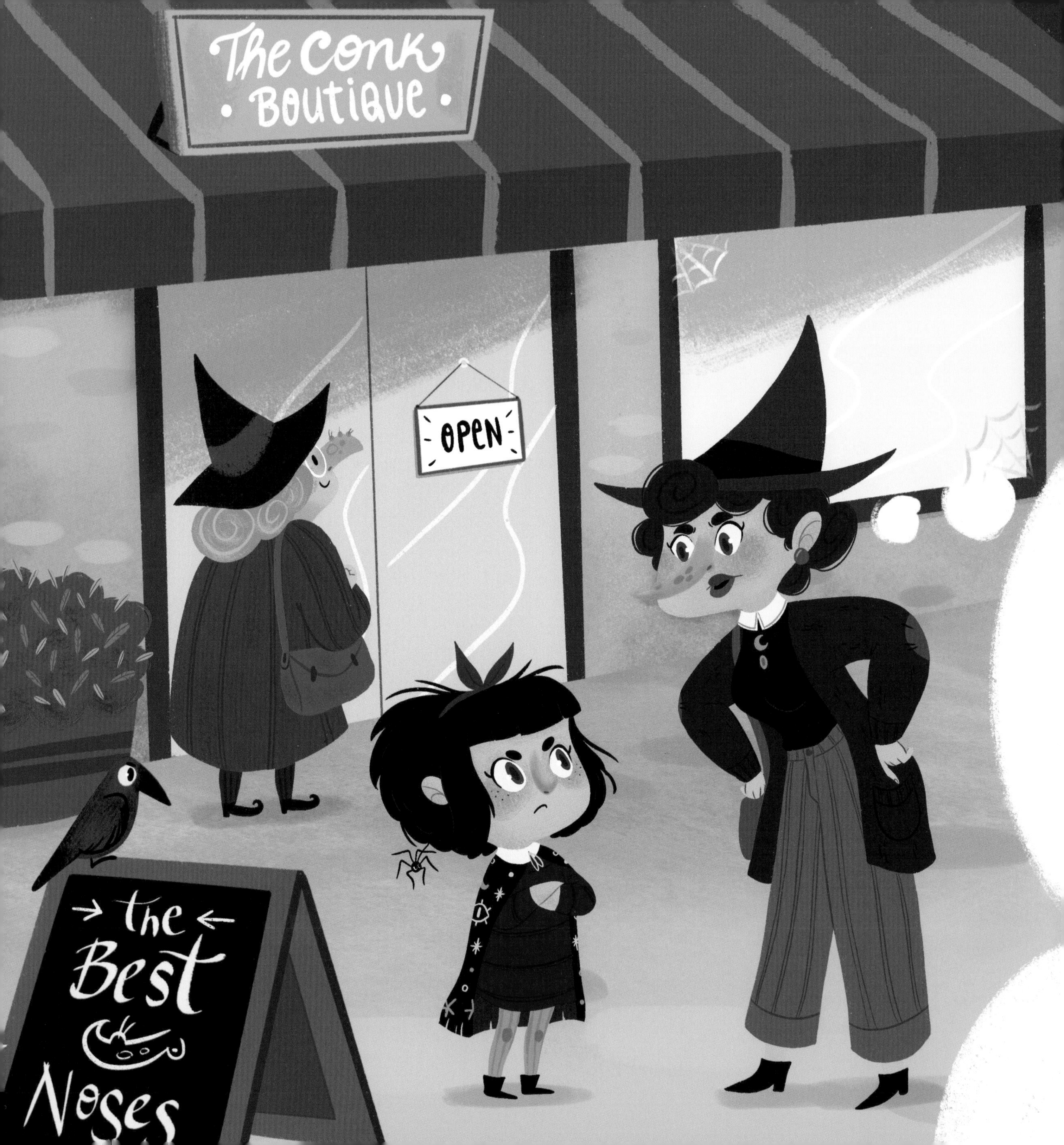
The Conk
• Boutique •
OPEN
the
Best
Noses

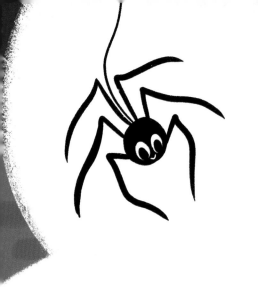

"Now Griz," says Mom, "**ENOUGH** of this!
I won't stand one more hitch!
You've **GOT** to choose a grown-up nose
To be a grown-up witch!"

"Says who?" says Griz and turns away,
Pretending not to care.

Then something shimmers in the light
And Griz can only stare.

"I've seen the nose I want," says Griz.
"My witch life starts **TODAY!**"
"At last!" says Mom, "Which nose is it?
I'll buy it right away!"

"Well," says Griz, "this nose won't ITCH
And ice cream will be fine.
Come here and have a look at it,
The nose I LOVE is...

...MINE!"

"But **NO** witch keeps her baby nose,
Oh Griz, this is the **WORST**."

"Hmmm," says Griz, "no witch you say?
Then I shall be the **FIRST**!"

So while most witches change their nose,
In search of witch perfection,

Griz feels grown-up and confident,
And **LOVES** her own reflection!